bug's life

Adapted by Jenny Miglis

In the grass beneath our feet, another world exists. . . .

Every year, the greedy grasshoppers forced the ants to work extra hard, collecting food for them. The ants had just finished, when the grasshoppers swarmed in.

On his way to the anthill, a young ant named Flik accidentally knocked over the offering stone with his latest harvesting invention. All the grain sank into a puddle in the riverbed below!

The angry grasshoppers invaded the anthill. "Where's my food?" Hopper, the grasshopper leader, snarled at the nervous ants. "We'll be back at the end of the season when the last leaf falls."

As quickly as they arrived, the grasshoppers disappeared.

The Queen ant met with her council to figure out what to do. There was no way the ants would be able to collect enough food for the grasshoppers *and* themselves before the rainy season!

"We could find bigger bugs to come here and fight, and forever rid us of Hopper and his gang!" Flik suggested. "I could travel to The City. I could search there."

The Council agreed to let Flik go. They realized that while the clumsy ant and his awkward inventions were gone, he couldn't cause any more trouble.

No sooner had Flik arrived at The City than he found the tough bugs he was looking for. A group of ex-circus performers was involved in a brawl with some rowdy flies.

Flik thought they were warrior bugs. "I have been scouting for bugs with your exact talents!" he told them. "My colony is in trouble. Please, will you help us?"

The circus bugs, who were looking for a new job, thought Flik was a talent scout—so they agreed.

When Flik and the circus bugs reached Ant Island, the ants held a welcome party. The youngest ants put on a play, acting out the upcoming battle with the grasshoppers.

The circus bugs realized there had been a misunderstanding. Rosie the spider whispered an explanation to Flik.

Flik couldn't believe his ears. He followed the bugs away from the rest of the colony. "Circus bugs?" he said with a gasp.

Just as the circus bugs were about to leave, a huge bird rose up from the grass behind them.

"Run!" Flik yelled.

"Look!" the ant princess Atta cried out. Her little sister, Princess Dot, was right in the hungry bird's path!

In a flash, Francis the ladybug flew into the air and grabbed Dot. The two tumbled into a crack in the riverbed.

The bird followed and began to peck at the crack.

Flik and the other circus bugs formed a rescue party. Heimlich the caterpillar distracted the bird, while Dim, a giant blue beetle, carried them all to safety.

"Hooray!" the ants cheered. The entire ant colony had seen the brave bugs rescue Princess Dot.

Princess Atta was very pleased with Flik. "Most bugs won't face a bird. Even Hopper's afraid of them!" she cried.

That gave Flik an idea. They could build a bird to scare off Hopper and his gang!

He took the circus bugs aside. "Keep pretending you're warriors," he told them. "You'll be gone before the grasshoppers ever arrive."

So, everyone got to work. Little by little, they constructed a bird out of leaves and twigs. When they had finished, they hoisted the bird into a tree.

"I've told everyone you'll be stationed deep in the command bunker," Flik whispered to the circus bugs. "I'll sneak you out the back way, and then you're out of here forever."

But the circus bugs didn't want to leave. They wanted to stay to help their new ant friends.

Just then, P.T. Flea, the circus bugs' old boss, arrived. He wanted to hire them back. "We'll be the top circus act in the business," he said.

"You mean, you're not warriors?" Princess Atta cried in disbelief. The ant colony sent the circus bugs—and Flik—away.

Soon after, the grasshoppers arrived and found out the ants did not have their grain. "Not one ant sleeps until we get every scrap of food on this island!" Hopper thundered.

Princess Dot ran to get help. She found Flik with the circus bugs. "You have to go back!" she cried.

After they all returned, Flik, Dot, and her friends launched the fake bird into the air. The grasshoppers dove for cover.

Even Hopper was frightened—until the bird caught fire! Now he knew that it wasn't a real bird. Hopper charged at Flik.

This time, the entire ant colony and the circus bugs charged back. They overpowered the small grasshopper gang. But then Hopper took Flik hostage!

Princess Atta rushed to the rescue. She grabbed Flik and flew the two of them away.

"Go that way! I've got an idea," Flik said.

Hopper followed the two ants right to where they wanted him. Just when Hopper thought he had them cornered, a big sparrow popped out of its nest. The grasshopper thought it was another trick. Not this time! The bird opened its beak and in one gulp, Hopper was gone.

Soon spring came to Ant Island. The circus bugs went on tour, bidding their ant friends farewell—until the next season.

"Bye!" the ants called. They would never have to fear the nasty grasshoppers again.